W9-CLI-018

What's in Aunt Mary's Room?

by Elizabeth Fitzgerald Howard
Illustrated by Cedric Lucas

Clarion Books/*New York*

Clarion Books
a Houghton Mifflin Company imprint
215 Park Avenue South, New York, NY 10003

Text copyright © 1996 by Elizabeth Fitzgerald Howard
Illustrations copyright © 1996 by Cedric Lucas

The illustrations were executed in pastel on Strathmore pastel paper.
The text was set in 16-point Goudy.

All rights reserved.

For information about permission to reproduce selections from this book, write to
Permissions, Houghton Mifflin Company, 215 Park Avenue South, New York, NY 10003.

www.houghtonmifflinbooks.com

Printed in U.S.A.

Library of Congress Cataloging-in-Publication Data

Howard, Elizabeth Fitzgerald.
What's in Aunt Mary's room? / by Elizabeth Fitzgerald Howard ; illustrated by Cedric Lucas.
p.   cm.
Summary: While visiting their Great-Aunt Flossie, two sisters get a chance
to see what family treasures are stored in a locked room there.
ISBN 0-395-69845-6   PA ISBN 0-618-24621-5
[1. Great-aunts—Fiction 2. Family—Fiction. 3. Sisters—Fiction. 4. Afro-Americans—
Fiction. 5. Baltimore (Md.)—Fiction.] I. Lucas, Cedric, ill. II Title.
PZ7.H83273Wh   1995
[E]—dc20   94-4985
CIP
AC

BVG   10 9 8 7 6 5 4 3 2

To the past:
Great-grandfather Thomas Bradford,
Great-aunt Mary Bradford,
Grandmother Sarah Elizabeth Bradford James,
Bertha James Fitzgerald (my mother),
and Sarah Florence James Wright (Aunt Flossie);
and to the future:
Jane, Susan, Laura, Jeffrey, Sarah, and Jonathan.
—E.F.H.

To Diane, Jorrell, Jaleesa, "Nana"
To all who inspire
—C.L.

Sarah and I have a game.
We call it "What's in Aunt Mary's Room?"
Once when we were riding in the car
Mommy told us about the real Aunt Mary's room
in Great-great-aunt Flossie's house.
Aunt Mary slept there, a long time ago.
Then, when Aunt Mary was ninety-eight, she died.
"Her room was empty," Mommy said.
"And Aunt Flossie began putting things there."
"What things?" I asked.
"Oh, I don't know," Mommy answered.
"Things to save, things to keep.
After a while, Aunt Mary's room was stuffed full,
and Aunt Flossie locked the door."

I wondered what was in Aunt Mary's room.
What were the things to save, the things to keep?
So Sarah and I made up a game.
We took turns thinking of things
that began with a, then b and c.
Funny, silly things, because we didn't know
what really was in Aunt Mary's room.
I told Aunt Flossie about our game
in a thank-you letter for my Christmas present.
She wrote me a letter too.
"Dear Susan, What a funny game! May I play?
Your cursive writing is very, very good.
Love, Aunt Flossie."

One Saturday afternoon when Mommy and Daddy
were driving us to Aunt Flossie's house,
I said, "OK, what's in Aunt Mary's room?"
"Alligators," said Sarah.
"Alligators and baby buggies," Daddy said.
"Alligators, baby buggies, and car seats," said Mommy.
"Alligators, baby buggies, car seats,
and Dairy Queens," I said,
because we were passing a Dairy Queen.
Everybody laughed and laughed
till we reached Aunt Flossie's house.
But I kept wondering, the way I always did.
What's really in Aunt Mary's room?

Sarah and I ran up Aunt Flossie's steps.
Aunt Flossie opened the door
and waved to Mommy and Daddy.
"We'll be back at five to go get crab cakes!"
Daddy said as they drove away.
"Susan, Sarah," said Aunt Flossie.

"I'm so glad to see you."
We sipped tea and ate cookies
the way we always do at Aunt Flossie's house.
Then Aunt Flossie said, "Girls, I need you to help me.
Today I want to go into Aunt Mary's room."

I looked at Sarah. She looked at me.
We said together, "Aunt Mary's room!"
"Aunt Flossie, we'll help you," I said.
"What's in Aunt Mary's room?" Sarah asked.
"Oh, things to save, things to keep," said Aunt Flossie.
"It's been a long time since I was in there.
First we need to find the key."
"It's not on the string with all your keys,
Aunt Flossie?" I asked.
"No, I put it somewhere in a safe place."
Aunt Flossie closed her eyes and thought a minute.
Then she said, "Girls, try the top drawer of the sideboard."

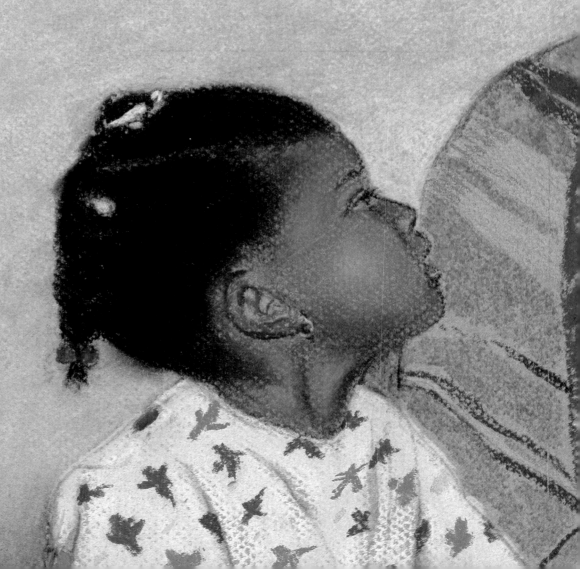

We opened the drawer.
Inside were forks and spoons and napkins
and pencils and place mats
and nutcrackers and old envelopes
and pictures of ladies with flowing dresses
and men with long beards.
"That's Uncle Jimmy.
He had such a fine, fine grocery store,"
Aunt Flossie said, pointing to one picture.
But we didn't see a key.
"Where else should we look, Aunt Flossie?" I asked.
Aunt Flossie closed her eyes again.
"Let's try the bookcases in the living room," she said.
"Somewhere there's a make-believe book
made for hiding things."

Aunt Flossie has so many books!
We looked on all the shelves till Sarah found it.
It looked like a book, but it was a secret box.
"Something's in here!" said Sarah.
She took a little soft bag out of the pretend book.
"Shake it," said Aunt Flossie.
Something shiny fell out.
"Oh, my," Aunt Flossie said.
"That's a five-dollar gold piece.
Must have been there a long, long time."
"But where's the key?" I asked.
"Where else can we look, Aunt Flossie?"
"Let's try my jewelry chest. It's upstairs
on the bureau in my room."

Sarah and I ran up to Aunt Flossie's bedroom.
All her hatboxes are there.
Thirty-seven. I always count them.
Aunt Flossie gave us her pink leather jewelry chest.
I found my favorite flower pin with the yellow petals
and the dark stone in the middle.
It looks like a black-eyed Susan.
I like it because I'm a black-eyed Susan, too.
Then I noticed a teeny tiny drawer in the jewelry chest.
"Aunt Flossie!" I shouted. "Here's a key!"
"Susan, that's it," Aunt Flossie said.
"I knew I had put it in a safe place."

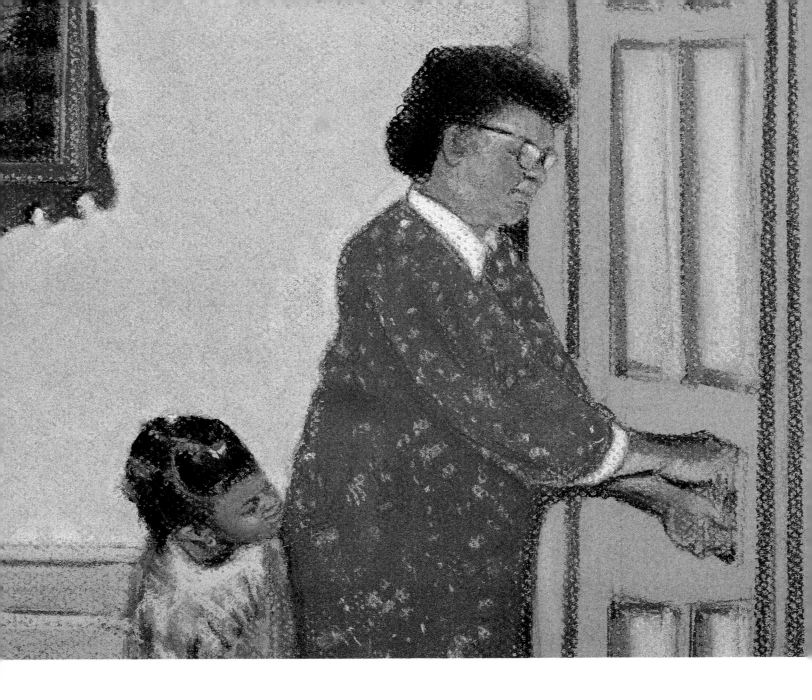

Sarah and I ran down the hall to Aunt Mary's old door.
Aunt Flossie followed us.
She poked the key into the lock and wiggled it around.
Sarah and I waited. Aunt Flossie turned the doorknob.

Slowly, slowly the door squeaked open.
And we were looking into Aunt Mary's room!
"It's dark," Sarah whispered.
I could see shadows and shapes. It was sort of scary.

Then Aunt Flossie turned on the light.
There were boxes and boxes and boxes!
And barrels.
There were chairs on top of chairs
and lamps and mirrors and flowerpots
and newspapers and magazines
and an old sewing machine,
and a big old bed with stuff piled on it
and more piles underneath.
"What are all those things?" I asked.
Aunt Flossie smiled. "Things to save.
Things to keep," she said.
She sounded really happy.
"Now I need someone who can climb."
"I can climb!" I said.
"I can climb, too!" Sarah said.
"Over on the other side of the room is a window.
In front of the window is a table," Aunt Flossie told us.
"On the table is a very large, very heavy book.
It's our family Bible. Do you suppose
you can find the Bible and bring it to me?"
"We can, we can, Aunt Flossie!" we said together.

Sarah and I took off our shoes
and climbed up on the big bed.
We squeezed between some boxes.
We stepped over onto the sewing machine
and down on the other side
and sideways to fit between a big box
and a big old chair.
Then I peeked around another big box.
"I see the window and the table!" I said.

"Do you see the Bible?" Aunt Flossie called.
Her voice seemed to come from far away.
"Something is wrapped up in an old towel,"
I said. I looked under the towel.
"Yes, there's an enormous gigantic book here."
"Wonderful, girls! You've found it,"
said Aunt Flossie. "Now, can you bring it here?"

I tried and Sarah tried to lift up the enormous book,
but we couldn't.
"It's too big, Aunt Flossie," I said.
"We can't carry it."
Sarah had a good idea. She said,
"Maybe we can pick it up in the towel."
"How can we climb back?" I asked.
Then I had a good idea, too.
"If we put it down on the floor,
I can push it under the bed."
"Be careful, girls," said Aunt Flossie's faraway voice.
"That Bible is precious."

The Bible was very, very heavy,
but we held the ends of the towel tightly
and slid it off the table and down to the floor.
I scrunched low and started pushing it.
Spiderwebs tickled my nose and I almost got stuck,
but I crawled and pushed
till the Bible and I came out the other side!
Sarah climbed back across the top of everything.
"Bravo!" said Aunt Flossie. "Bravo!
You girls are both heroes!
Now I want to show you something."

We pulled the towel with the precious Bible
to Aunt Flossie's room.
She sat in a chair while we unwrapped it.
I read the words on the cover.

*"Presented to Thomas Bradford
with thanks from Bethel A.M.E. Church,
Baltimore, January 20, 1859."*

"That's your great-great-great-grandpa.
My grandfather," Aunt Flossie said.
"He helped raise money
for Bethel African Methodist Episcopal Church."
"Can we look inside?" asked Sarah.
"Yes," said Aunt Flossie.
"Open where the ribbon bookmark is."
We opened to the place very carefully.
We found a dried flower
and some pages with names and dates
in fancy cursive writing.
"That's our family," Aunt Flossie said.
"It's an important record
of an African American family,
and I wanted you to know about it.
Aunt Mary is there, and Uncle Jimmy,
and I'm there."
"Are we in it?" Sarah asked.
"Not yet," said Aunt Flossie. "Not yet.
But someone with your name is there, Sarah."
We found it on a page that said *Births:
Sarah Elizabeth Bradford, September 5, 1853.*
"She was my mother," said Aunt Flossie,
"and your great-great-grandma."

"Is my name there, Aunt Flossie?" I asked.
"Well, Susan," Aunt Flossie said,
"your name will be in the Bible very soon.
Since your handwriting is so clear and neat,
you may write down your name and Sarah's.
I'll show you where."
"Can I really write in this precious Bible,
Aunt Flossie?" I asked. I could hardly believe it.
"Certainly," said Aunt Flossie,

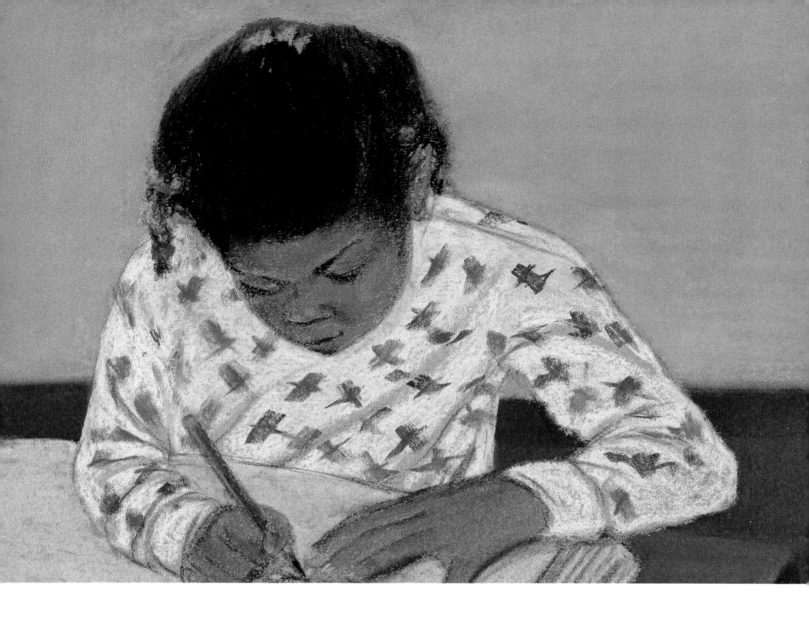

and she pulled a pen from her pocket.
Sarah and I lifted the heavy Bible up in the towel
and swung it over to a low table.
Slowly, slowly—I didn't even breathe—
I wrote my name and my birthday,
and I wrote Sarah's name and her birthday.
"Very, very nice, Susan," said Aunt Flossie.
She smiled at me.
I felt really proud.

We sat all quiet for a minute.
Then Sarah said, "Is it five o'clock yet?"
"My, my," Aunt Flossie said.
"Your parents will be here soon,
and I think I'm getting hungry."
It's amazing, but I had forgotten
about crab cakes!
"Let's play our game while we're waiting," I said.
"What's in Aunt Mary's room?"
"Antique armchairs," said Aunt Flossie.
"Antique armchairs and a big Bible," said Sarah.
"Antique armchairs, a big Bible,
and crab cakes!" I said.
We were still laughing
when Mommy and Daddy rang the doorbell.